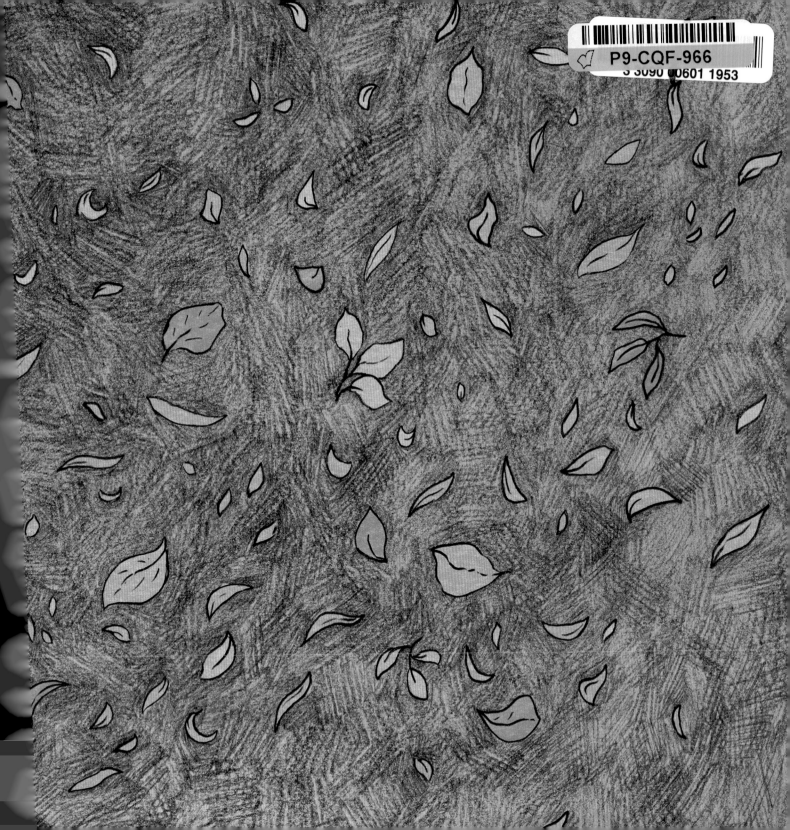

For my friends Alicia Kobayashi and
Rodrigo Morlesin — JB

Para Jairo y sus historias
For Jairo and his stories — RY

Lion and Mouse

Written by
Jairo Buitrago

Pictures by
Rafael Yockteng

Translated by
Elisa Amado

Groundwood Books
House of Anansi Press
Toronto Berkeley

In the woods there lived a very lovely lion who was like a sun, and a small mouse who was a busybody and a glutton.

One day, the mouse marched into the lion's house without being invited.

Being well mannered, he wiped his feet on the lion's mane.

Before he could leave without saying goodbye, the lion grabbed him.

"Where are you going, breakfast?" the lion asked him.

"Breakfast?" said the mouse. "Don't eat me today, please. I'm off to see my girlfriend."

"Someone as small and ugly as you couldn't have a girlfriend."

"But I do! And if you let me go I might be able to return the favor."

"HAH, HAH, HAH, HAH, HAH!" laughed the lion as only lions can. "Such an insignificant little animal as you is going to return the favor? Get out."

And the mouse ran away.

"Insignificant" means being of no use or importance and is the most insulting thing you could say about a mouse.

The next day, the lion went out for a walk and found a very handsome ham hanging from a tree.

It was a hunter's trap. And he fell into it.

In those days, people were foolish and hunted lions.

As the lion was crying, the mouse appeared. But the lion didn't recognize him because all mice looked alike to him.

"It's me, Mr. Lion," the mouse said. "Yesterday's mouse."

"And what do you want?"

"I can rescue you from your trap."

The lion felt like laughing again, but it didn't seem like such a good idea just then.

The mouse bit through the net that was covering the lion and freed him.

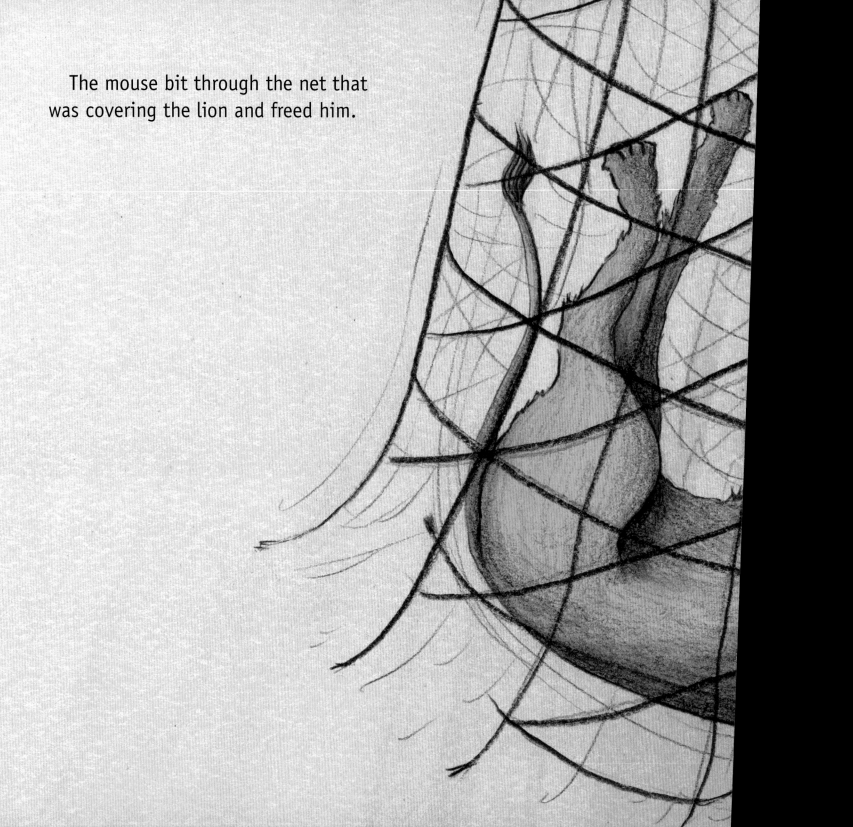

The lion was astonished. He had been rescued by someone so small?

"I told you I'd return the favor," exclaimed the mouse before he fled into the bushes.

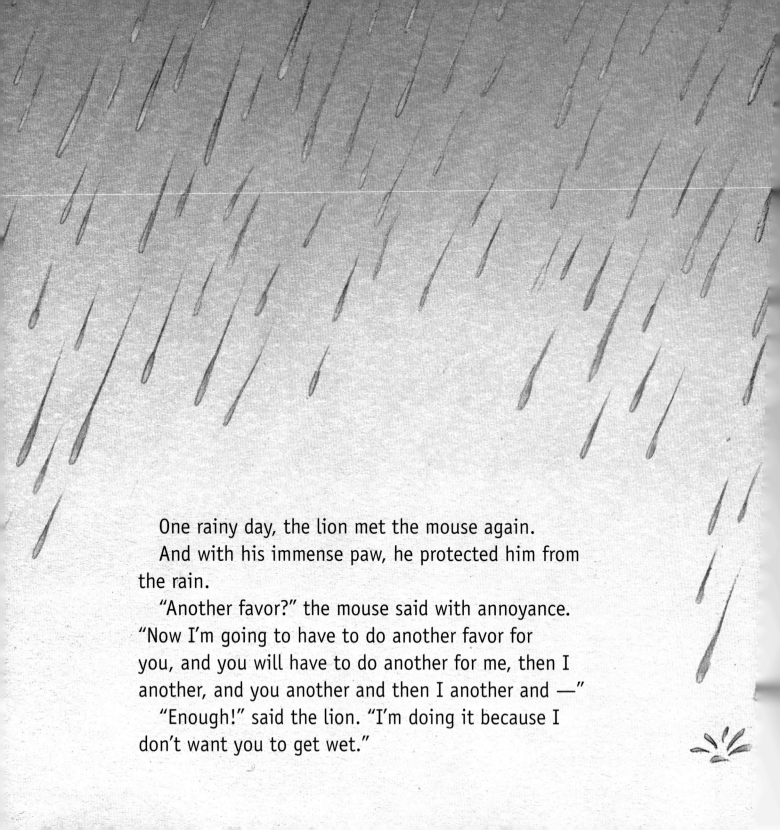

One rainy day, the lion met the mouse again.

And with his immense paw, he protected him from the rain.

"Another favor?" the mouse said with annoyance. "Now I'm going to have to do another favor for you, and you will have to do another for me, then I another, and you another and then I another and —"

"Enough!" said the lion. "I'm doing it because I don't want you to get wet."

And that is how they began to be good to each other.

These weren't favors. They didn't do this because
they expected to get something back.

They ended up living together in the lion's house, because there was more room there than in the mouse's home.

One day, the lion went up very, very close to the mouse, to see him better.

"You know, seeing you so close up, friend mouse, you aren't at all, not at all ugly."

They lived together nicely the rest of their days in the woods they loved so much.

The lion walked through the bushes with his good mouse sitting on his head.

Originally published as *Léon y ratón* by Cataplum Libros in 2017
Text copyright © 2017 by Jairo Buitrago
Illustrations copyright © 2017 by Rafael Yockteng
Translation copyright © 2019 by Elisa Amado
Published in Canada and the USA in 2019 by Groundwood Books

Groundwood Books / House of Anansi Press
groundwoodbooks.com

We gratefully acknowledge the Government of Canada for its financial
support of our publishing program.

With the participation of the Government of Canada
Avec la participation du gouvernement du Canada | Canadä

Library and Archives Canada Cataloguing in Publication
Buitrago, Jairo
[León y ratón. English]
Lion and mouse / written by Jairo Buitrago; pictures by Rafael Yockteng;
translated by Elisa Amado.
Translation of: León y ratón.
Based on the fable by Aesop.
Issued in print and electronic formats.
ISBN 978-1-77306-224-2 (hardcover).— ISBN 978-1-77306-225-9 (PDF)
I. Aesop II. Yockteng, Rafael, illustrator III. Amado, Elisa, translator
IV. Title. V. Title: León y ratón. English.
PZ8.2.B85Li 2019   j398.24'529757   C2018-904231-1
C2018-904232-X

The mixed-media illustrations were created with
an 8B pencil with color added digitally.
Art direction and design by Ana Carolina Palmero
Printed and bound in Malaysia

MIX
Paper from
responsible sources
FSC® C012700

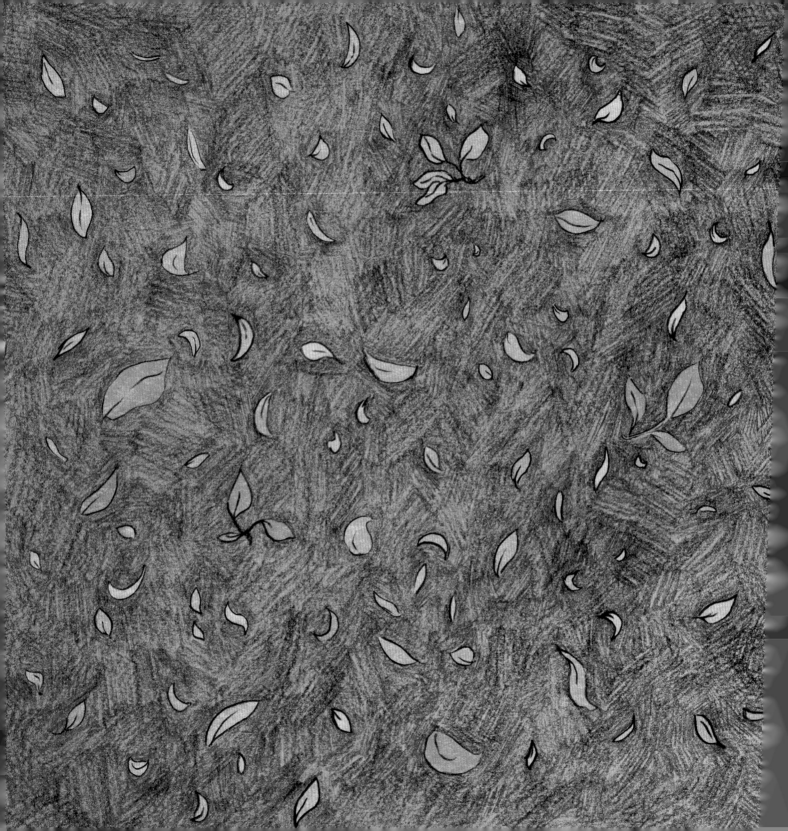